32 children killed, 67 wounded. I do not need to consult a search engine, I know these numbers by heart. It's currently the tenth day of the war, and this is official information that has been made public, but the Russian aggressor is bombing cities, towns, roads and villages in all regions of my country, and I am painfully aware that this figure is increasing.

I wrote this book about different children from different Ukrainian families in 2017, when Crimea was annexed and part of the Donetsk and Luhansk regions of Ukraine were temporarily occupied by the Russian Federation. I am writing this introduction from the corridor where we are hiding with my mother, who survived World War II as a child, and my dog, because there is another missile threat over the Kyiv sky.

I imagine that someone from Maya's class is now praying in a bomb shelter, someone else just wants Dad to be alive, and Mum to come back from police patrol. Another person has already lost a loved one. Some spent more than five days travelling to another country, some are crying as they sit in an unfamiliar town, and some are rereading *Harry Potter* and believing in magic that protects children.

War is always catastrophic for children. I want to shout that the children of my country need international protection. They have the right to a present and a future in which they are not under siege or occupation, not in a bomb shelter, not under fire, but in safe and peaceful homes, surrounded by loving families. The world needs to understand this.

Larysa Denysenko

First published in Ukraine in 2017 by Vydavnytstvo
First published in the UK in 2022 by Studio Press Books,
an imprint of Bonnier Books UK,
4th floor, Victoria House, Bloomsbury Square, London
WC1B 4DA
Owned by Bonnier Books,
Sveavägen 56, Stockholm, Sweden

www.bonnierbooks.co.uk

Original text copyright © Larysa Denysenko 2017
English text translation copyright © Burshtyna Tereshchenko 2022
Illustrations copyright © Masha Foya 2017
Originally published in the Ukrainian language by Vydavnytstvo © 2017

Printed by Livonia Print, Latvia

1 3 5 7 9 10 8 6 4 2

ISBN 978-1-80078-414-7

A CIP catalogue for this book is available
from the British Library

LARYSA DENYSENKO · MASHA FOYA

MAYA
and HER FRIENDS

ACKNOWLEDGEMENTS

Livonia Print, being Climate Neutral and a socially responsible company, in response to Bonnier's call for support of Ukrainian children, sponsored the production, production consumables and transportation costs of this edition.

This book is printed on Lessebo Design, donated by Lessebo Paper. Lessebo Design is one of the most climate friendly paper qualities in the world and is the only paper Cradle to Cradle Certified © at Gold level.

All publisher profits will be donated to charities helping to protect the children of Ukraine.

My name is Maya. It's important! Please, don't call me May, because May is a month and I'm human. Sometimes people call me May-may or even Mimi. But I'm only OK with that if you're my friend, or one of my parents or if I really like you! What's your name?

I love cat ear buns, the colour green and macaroni and cheese. And rabbits and pugs. And also witch dolls and summer. And watermelons! Lots of them. What about you? What do you like?

I'm in year five. There are seventeen of us in the class. Mostly we get along brilliantly, but sometimes we fight. And quarrel. And joke around. Or sulk and pout. Or get offended by someone. All together, or one at a time.

Sometimes we are overcome by the "tranda"! Miss Yulia, our teacher, invented this word herself. It's what happens when we get naughty and sleepy and don't want to do anything. Has this ever happened to you? The only way to defeat the "tranda" is to smile, and tell jokes and interesting stories. I like to tell spooky or silly stories.

SOPHIYA and SOLOMIA

Sophiya is one of my best friends. We call her Sophy the First. There are three Sophiyas in our class, which can get confusing if you're not careful. Three Sophiyas can cause some serious sophiyahavoc!

Sophiya the First has a twin sister called Solomia, or Solya. We used to call them test-tube babies, but then Miss Yulia explained that Sophiya the First and Solomia are just like us.

I already knew that, though, because my friend is the realest one there is!

Not all adults can have their own kids. Sophiya and Sol's mum and dad couldn't, so they asked their doctors to help them. Their aunt donated her egg so that Sophiya the First and Solya could be born. And a man donated his sperm, but he is a mystery – a bit like a secret agent! Only the doctors know who he is.

Miss Yulia told us that people who donate their eggs and sperm are called donors.

SOPHIYA THE SECOND

At first, Sophiya the Second also wanted to be called Sophiya the First, but that would have been very confusing for everyone!

Sophiya the Second has one dad and two mums. She lives with her dad and her second mum, because her first mum lives very far away, in Australia. It's a whole separate country-continent – an island country. Sophiya the Second never calls her second mum a step-mum, because in fairytales step-mums are often mean, but her second mum is incredibly kind.

Australian mum always sends Sophiya the Second
postcards with kangaroos, koalas and platypuses
on them. These are adorable creatures that live in
Australia – you can't help but want to kiss them and
squeeze them and be friends with them!

SOPHIYA THE THIRD

Sophiya the Third wasn't in reception with us. She's new! She and her mum came from Luhansk.

Sophiya the Third's dad has gone missing. People often do when there's a war[*].

[*] There are now several million displaced Ukrainian people, which is more than the population of many countries, such as Norway. Since 2014, Ukraine has been conducting an Anti-Terrorist Operation and is trying to get people back to their homes. Sophiya the Third and her mother were forced to move to Kyiv from Luhansk, because their city was under temporary occupation. But Russia did not stop there, and in 2022 waged war on Ukraine.

FATHER

Sophiya the Third and her mum believe that they will be able to find Sophiya's dad. We believe it, too!

Every war must come to an end someday, and people ought to be searched for, until they are found.

DANYLKO

Danylko lives with his mum. He has no idea where his father is. But his father didn't go missing during the war, he disappeared before Danylko was even born.

Danylko's mum isn't looking for his dad. You see, sometimes people just don't want to be found.

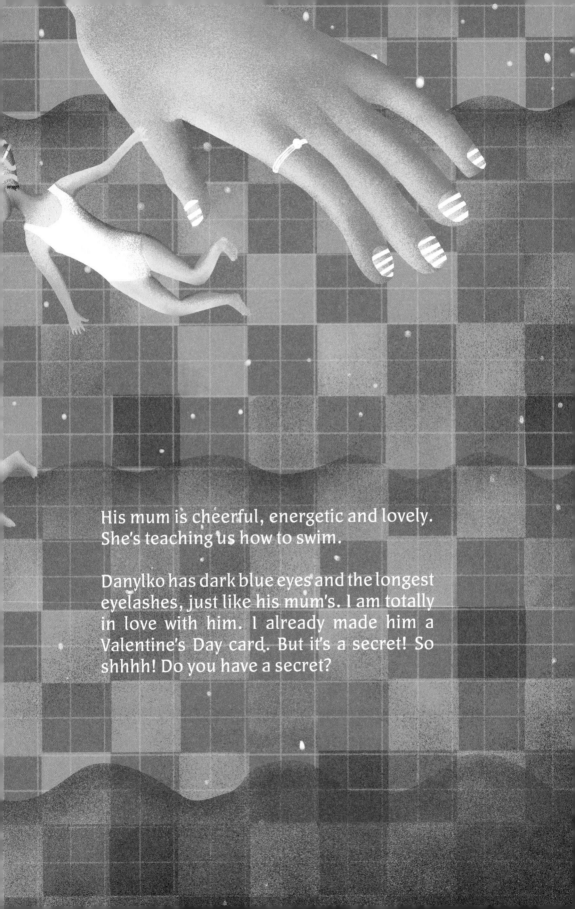

His mum is cheerful, energetic and lovely. She's teaching us how to swim.

Danylko has dark blue eyes and the longest eyelashes, just like his mum's. I am totally in love with him. I already made him a Valentine's Day card. But it's a secret! So shhhh! Do you have a secret?

AKSANA

People often call Aksana "Oksana", which isn't right. Miss Yulia taught us that names are very important. Every child has a right to their own name, and people should respect this right and make sure they don't change the name in any way.

Different countries have similar names, but they can be spelled and pronounced differently. For example, here in Ukraine, we have the name Olesya, or Lesya. But in Belarus, they have Alyesya and Lyesya.

Aksana lives with her dad because her mum died. She misses her mum terribly and sometimes cries. Miss Yulia once asked Aksana if she remembers what her mum's favourite flower was. Aksana told her that it was hollyhocks. Now we have yellow hollyhocks growing near our school, so we can remember Aksana's mum. We all planted them together. Now, whenever Aksana sees hollyhocks, she smiles. It's important to remember the people we love.

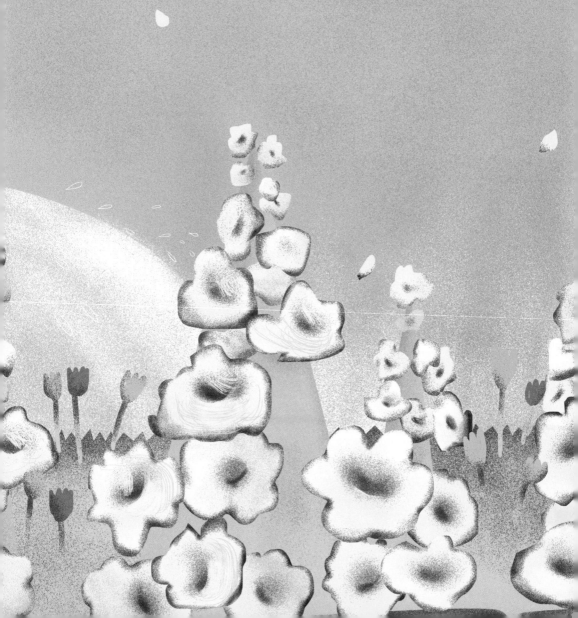

HRYSTYNA

Hrystyna lives with her grandma. Her mother works in Italy as a housemaid, and her father works as a butcher in the United Kingdom. Italy and the United Kingdom are two big European countries, just like Ukraine!

Hrystyna used to be bullied and called names, like "Skype kid" or "orphan".

But Miss Yulia explained that you must never behave arrogantly, and you must always be kind. Every kid has their own story and their own family. Just because somebody's life is different from yours, that is no excuse for sneering and bullying.

Hrystyna talks to her parents on Skype. She also teaches her daddy lots of English words. And her daddy always forgets that a sheep's child is called a "lamb". Or, perhaps, he just pretends to forget, to make Hrystyna laugh.

How many Ukrainian words do you know? What about French? Or maybe even Russian?

KYRYLO

Kyrylo isn't an orphan. He has a mother and a father, but the state took away their parental rights as they weren't looking after him properly. Once, Kyrylo almost died in a house fire because his parents left him home alone and completely forgot about him! But the firemen rescued Kyrylo.

The state placed Kyrylo in an orphanage, but he was miserable there. You see, in the orphanage, lots of things weren't allowed – like choosing toys, reading magazines about different countries or putting your hair in a tiny ponytail, just like the famous footballer, David Beckham.

Last year, Kyrylo got a mentor. His name is Borys, and he is amazing! He helps and supports Kyrylo with everything. He truly became his family.

Thanks to Borys, Kyrylo came to our school and didn't have to continue to study in the orphanage. Borys often visits us and tells us about different countries. He works in a travel agency, so he travels a lot.

Kyrylo wants to become an adventurer. So do I. What about you? Do you like travelling?

NASTYA and NAZAR

Nastya and Nazar came to reception together. They have been friends since birth, because they are first cousins. They live in the same house, together with their grandma, Nastya's mum and Nazar's mum.

Nastya's and Nazar's mums are sisters. They look very much alike: both have curly ginger hair.

Meanwhile, Nastya and Nazar are nothing alike.
They have inherited their fathers' appearances. But
their mums and their grandma never talk about
their dads. Nastya believes that her
father is dead, and Nazar
thinks that his father is
working abroad.

They have a very nice family and I really enjoy visiting them. You see, Nastya is my other best friend. And their granny always treats us to the tastiest curd fritters. They are simply wonderful!

TYMKO

Tymko lives with his mum and her new boyfriend one week, and with his dad the next – they take turns. Tymko always remembers who he's going to be living with each week, but his parents often get confused about whose turn it is and forget to pick him up from school. When this happens, Miss Yulia takes Tymko home, or he goes home with someone else in class. Miss Yulia is always sending notes to his parents, to tell them that they shouldn't forget about him. But they still do, and they feel very bad afterwards and apologise a lot.

Tymko's mother plays the violin and her boyfriend plays the guitar. Tymko's dad is a singer at the Opera House. Whenever the three of them get together, they always put on a real show. But it doesn't happen very often as they are all busy with their own lives.

Miss Yulia says that Tymko brings them all together. This makes Tymko feel very good.

YEVA

Yeva is the best at maths. Maybe that's because her step-dad works in a bank!

Once, he came to our class and taught us how to plan a weekly budget. He showed us how to work out what we could spend, and how much to save up, as well as what kind of gifts we could give each other and which ones are too expensive.

Yeva gets along well with her step-dad, and he loves her dearly. Still, Yeva wonders whether he will still love her as much when her mummy has a new baby, because this baby will be his real daughter.

But Miss Yulia told us that true love isn't just for people who are related by blood. I believe in true love.

TAYA and LEVKO

I can see that such love exists when I look at Taya, her brother Levko and their family.

Levko knows nothing about his dad. His mum gave birth to him and then never wanted to see him again. All he knows is that she exists somewhere. And she knows that he exists somewhere, too.

When Levko was just a baby, he lived in a special home for infants. Later, he was transferred to an orphanage. But then Taya's mum and dad adopted him, and Taya became his sister.

Don't you even try to tell Levko that Taya isn't his real sister, or Taya will teach you a lesson!

RAYIS

Rayis moved to Kyiv from Dzhankoi. Dzhankoi is a town in Crimea. Rayis used to live in a house surrounded by a peach garden. It sounds lovely! But now he lives in a rented one-bedroom apartment with his dad, mum, two sisters and his auntie. He often gets quite sad*.

Rayis is a Crimean Tatar. Crimean Tatars are indigenous people of Ukraine, which means that historically they originated from Crimea. Once, when Ukraine was part of the Soviet Union, Crimean Tatars were forced out of Crimea and were forbidden to return. They were robbed of their homes, their land and their country. It was horrible and very painful.

Crimean Tatars started returning to Crimea when the Soviet Union began to crumble, and the new and independent Ukraine was being born. They rebuilt their homes – Rayis and his family did the same, but now they have lost their home for a second time.

* In February 2014, countless "green people" landed on the Crimean peninsula in Ukraine. They were Russian military and mercenaries in camouflage uniforms who forcibly took over Ukrainian territory. That's how Rayis's house ended up being on occupied land. At this very moment, perhaps other people are living in his home – people who have no right to be there. Ukraine officially proclaimed 20th February 2014 the beginning of the occupation of Crimea by the Russian Federation.

By the way, Rayis has a monobrow! That's when your eyebrows meet above your eyes. It looks just like a tiny bird. We used to giggle at that, but Miss Yulia explained that laughing at someone's appearance is silly, because we are all different. It's the same as making fun of my upturned nose, or taunting Sophiya the Second for her freckles, or mocking Danylko because of his big ears.
We felt very bad.

And then Miss Yuliya showed us pictures of an artist called Frida Kahlo. She is gorgeous, talented and famous. And she also has a monobrow!

PETRO

Petro has a family, but he also belongs to a clan! And he knows lots about his clan because he is constantly being told stories about it. You see, Petro is a Romani.

Petro's mother and father aren't the only ones who come to parents' evening. Sometimes, the oldest woman in the clan comes instead. At first, we thought she was his granny, but she isn't. Whenever she lectures Petro, he listens to her intently. There are a lot of people who can lecture Petro! But then again, he also gets way more presents.

We are proud of Petro because he won a singing contest.

МАЯ

MAYA

I can sing, too, but I'm not as
good as Petro. My mums say
that I sing like an angel.

My name is Maya, and I have two mums. People often wonder why that is, but there's nothing unusual about it! I have no dad: he is a secret donor. But my mums are not secret – they are very real. And they love each other, and me.

Пані Юлія

Майя

Софія 1

Соломія

Софія 2

Софія 3

Данилко

Аксана

Христина

Кирило

Назар

Настя

Тимко

Єва

Левко

Тая

Раїс

Петро

Miss Yulia says that children should live amongst love.

It doesn't matter if you are part of a tiny family or a huge clan, if you are related by blood or not, or even how many mums or dads you have. The most important thing is to love and respect one another. Those are the most important values.

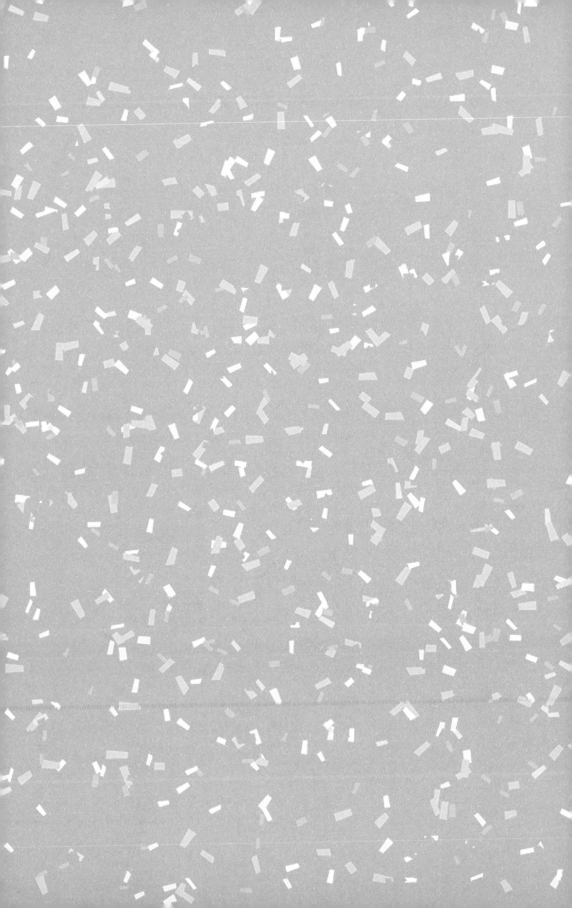